The Sleepover Club

Have you been invited to all these sleepovers?

Sleepover Club Blitz

by Angie Bates

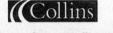

Collins

An imprint of HarperCollinsPublishers

The Sleepover Club ® is a
registered trademark of HarperCollins*Publishers* Ltd

First published in Great Britain by Collins in 2000
Collins is an imprint of HarperCollins*Publishers* Ltd
77-85 Fulham Palace Road, Hammersmith,
London, W6 8JB

The HarperCollins website address is
www.**fire**and**water**.com

3 5 7 9 8 6 4

Text copyright © Angie Bates 2000

Original series characters, plotlines
and settings © Rose Impey 1997

ISBN 0 00675507 0

The author asserts the moral right to
be identified as the author of the work.

Printed and bound in Great Britain by
Omnia Books Limited,
Glasgow G64

Sleepover Kit List

1. Sleeping bag
2. Pillow
3. Pyjamas or a nightdress
4. Slippers
5. Toothbrush, toothpaste, soap etc
6. Towel
7. Teddy
8. A creepy story
9. Food for a midnight feast:
   chocolate, crisps, sweets, biscuits.
   In fact anything you like to eat.
10. Torch
11. Hairbrush
12. Hair things like a bobble or hairband,
    if you need them
13. Clean knickers and socks
14. Change of clothes for the next day
15. Sleepover diary and membership card

CHAPTER ONE

ATISHOO! Oops! Didn't mean to sneeze on you! Oh, I don't believe it. It's you!

No, it's great. I'm just embarrassed. You've caught me in my icky dog-walking clothes. I hadn't expected to run into any Sleepover fans today. I must look a total mess.

Hang on, I've got to blow my nose. As you can see, I've got the WORST cold. My big sister, Tiffany, is threatening to enter me for the sneezing Olympics!

Oh, *now* I get the picture! A little bird leaked the news of our most outrageous sleepover since records began and you're desperate for an update, right?

Well, it might not look like it, but you *definitely* came to the right girl. Yep, the amazingly groovy Rosie Cartwright gets a starring role again! Yes, I DO mean me, you fluff-brain!

Unfortunately, you've caught me at a bad moment. Not only am I looking a scruffbag, but also (yikes, this sounds incredibly rude), I was just on my way out!! Is that bad luck or what?

Literally FIVE minutes before you showed up, I promised Mum I'd take our dog for a run. Jenny has the MOST energy. It's all I can do to keep up, while she drags me uphill and down whatever, chasing cute, fluffy (and totally imaginary) rabbits. Not the ideal situation for a girly chat, as I'm sure you'll agree.

It's such a pain. I'd heaps rather talk to you than walk our dog. No, I CAN'T take her later. The poor thing's been crossing her legs for hours.

Strictly speaking, it was my big sister's turn. I only agreed to do a swap on one condition. The absolute MICRO-second I get back, Tiffany has to march into that kitchen and make me a mega bowl of her dee-licious toffee-flavoured popcorn! Time-travel makes you incredibly hungry for some reason.

Sorry, I couldn't resist dropping that in! You should see your face! You think I'm kidding, don't you? Oh, come on. Don't tell me you've never wanted to go back in time, because I won't believe you!

The other day, all of us girls in the Sleepover Club shared our secret time-travel fantasies.

Lyndz, who is totally horse-mad, if you remember, wanted to go back to before Columbus. She said she'd just LURVE to see what America looked like before white men turned up with their guns and chicken-pox germs and stuff. "I'd hang out with Native Americans, and ride bareback on those gorgeous pinto ponies they had," she said.

Fliss wanted to go back to when girls wore Empire-line dresses, and those gauzy little shawls. I'm not saying Fliss is a bimbo or anything, but sometimes she really gives that impression!

"Could we have a teensy bit more info?" Kenny grinned. "Like when was this, exactly?"

Fliss looked vague. "I don't know. They put

their hair up in this really sweet style, and they visited each other's houses the whole time. Ooh, and the men stomped about in serious riding boots and swishy jackets, looking incredibly gorgeous."

It turned out Fliss had once caught an episode of *Pride and Prejudice* on TV, and fallen mushily in love with Mr Darcy!

Kenny's choice was SO not romantic. She wanted to be whisked back to 1966, purely so she could see England win the World Cup...

Frankie didn't fancy the past, full stop. "I'm not interested in stuff that's, like – OVER,"she said dramatically. "It's what's coming *next* that I'm interested in. Like, how soon can I travel to other planets?"

Personally, I'd like to be one of those feisty girls in the days of the Wild West. They could turn their hand to anything. Like, one minute they'd be making blueberry pie. And next thing, they'd grab a gun and blast away at some wild bear who'd started guzzling the family's maple syrup supply.

But what's all this got to do with *actual* time-travel, I hear you cry?

Yikes! Jenny's practically pulling my arm off. Sorry, but I'm going to have to go.

Tell you what! I've had a great idea. (If you're up for it, that is?)

Could we meet up back at my house later? Not only would that give me a chance to change into something a bit less doggy, but you'll have my undivided attention. You can even share my popcorn, if you like.

What do you mean, can't I give you a tiny hint before I go? Boy, you readers show no mercy!

OK. Here's a Sleepover mini-trailer to keep you going.

Picture one of those old-style newsreels, with that insanely cheerful male newsreader yelling over brass-band music.

SOUND OF WAILING SIRENS.

"Do you believe in time travel? You'd better! Because those five spunky Sleepover girls have just been back to the tremendously inspiring days of Spitfires, gas masks and ration books. Watch them dig for victory. Hear them warble about bluebirds over the white cliffs of Dover. Laugh aloud as they try to find the outside toilet in the black-out. Find out what happens when our intrepid heroines give up the home comforts of the twenty-first century for one entire weekend, and drop in on (BOOM! CRASH!! CRUMP!!!) the Second World War – for REAL!"

Yes, I am feeling perfectly well, thank you very much.

No, I'm not making it up!

But like I said, if you REALLY want to know what happened, come back and meet me after tea, OK?

Till then, TTFN! I'll translate later – gotta dash!!

CHAPTER TWO

You came back! That's SO sweet. I was worried my disgusting germs might put you off. Actually, I think the fresh air blew my cobwebs away. I'm feeling heaps better now. Plus, I've got all my stupid chores out of the way.

Me and Tiff really have to pull our weight since Dad walked out, otherwise poor Mum would end up doing everything herself. Also, if you remember, my older brother, Adam, has cerebral palsy. He'd help out if he could (in some moods, anyway!). But where walking the dog is concerned, he's not exactly a serious contender.

Anyway, the good news is, I'm finally free to

chill out with our favourite fan!! That's YOU, dumbo… Hope you noticed I swapped the doggy jogging pants for some stylish leisure wear? Us Sleepover girls have our reputations to keep up, you know!

My room feels cosy and welcoming, doesn't it? It used to be the pits. I HATED coming up here. Every time I walked in, I'd find myself getting all uptight about Dad leaving Mum to cope with this like, HUGE falling-down house, all by herself.

Don't tell anyone, but I think I went a bit off my rocker, those first few months. Maybe that's why, when I first joined the Sleepover Club, I did everything I could to put the others off sleeping over at our place.

Back then I was convinced my new friends would despise me if they ever found out what a dump I lived in. Luckily they totally refused to take any notice! And I'm really glad now.

Not only were those sleepovers a real laugh (everyone just LURVES staying at our place, for some reason), but I think they improved its vibes or something, because the atmosphere has completely changed for the better.

During one of our sleepovers, my friends helped me redecorate it in my favourite colours. Now it's my favourite place in the whole house. And boy! Since we came back from the 1940s it seems like total bedroom-heaven.

OK, keep your hair on – I'll get around to the time-travel thing eventually. First, I want to let you into a big secret. An incredibly embarrassing secret, actually.

It's about this boy.

This boy that I (I'm going to whisper it, OK?) – this boy I briefly, erm, gulp (eek, this is ridiculous!) – OK, here goes! This boy I really fancied.

YOU'RE shocked! Imagine how *I* felt!

Look, don't panic, OK – I got over it in next to no time, so I can still wear my BOYS ARE YUCK T-shirt with pride. But for two whole lessons, I truly thought I was in L.U.R.V.E.

Is that scary or what!! Still don't believe me? OK, I'll give you an idea how bad it was. Would you believe an ordinary school day could feel as deliciously cool as Saturday morning hooked up to *Live & Kicking* and chomping your favourite brand of jelly beans? Me neither!

Then, one morning Owen Cartwright walked into our classroom – and I almost fell off my chair in awe.

I know what you're thinking. This is not the gutsy girl you know and love, right? What can possibly have caused such a dramatic turn-around?

Well, first you should know that Owen is so-o good looking it's unbelievable. He's a total Prince William look-alike – except that Owen's more your footballer type, if you get me. But he's got that same floppy fair hair and amazing dark eyelashes. His eyes are hazel with gold flecks in. He's also got this dreamy little smile hovering round his mouth, which gives the impression he's smiling at these really deep private thoughts.

I don't know if the others told you, but recently our regular class teacher, Mrs Weaver, has been away on a course. So we've been having this supply teacher, Miss Pearson. When she introduced Owen to the whole class, I was so dazed, all I could think was: Wow, if me and Owen got married, I wouldn't even have to change my surname. And I leaned my chin on my hand and went into a total dream. (I told you this was embarrassing.)

Then I noticed something spooky. All the girls in the class were leaning their chins dreamily on *their* hands, too. All right, not Kenny. But that's only because she's got her image to keep up. Inside, she had turned to fluffy marshmallow like the rest of us.

No prizes for guessing the hot topic at break.

"I can't believe it!" Fliss shrieked. "He was looking at me all through maths. I thought I was going to DIE!" She went bright pink at the memory.

OK, you're thinking, no cause for alarm here! So what if Fliss did go soppy over some boy with a cute face? That's just Flissy, right?

Wrong wrong WRONG! This was something WAY bigger.

Ever heard of a thing called "charisma"? I looked it up in the dictionary, in case you're interested, and it means, "the special magnetic appeal, charm or power of an individual".

Well, that's Owen Cartwright to a T. He wasn't just cute-looking. He didn't just have this like, effortless cool. He had CHARISMA. And when girls saw him, even groovy streetwise girls like my mates, they totally lost it. They were like pitiful little iron filings, being sucked into a major magnetic field.

Boy, you should have seen the dirty look Frankie gave Fliss!

"Owen was looking at YOU?" she snapped. "Erm, I don't *think* so, Flissy. Didn't you see how when my ruler accidentally slipped out of my hand, Owen immediately handed it back? And he gave me this really gorgeous smile!" Frankie gave a big breathy sigh.

"Accidentally slipped, eh?" mused Kenny.

"Ooh, liar, liar!" spluttered Lyndz. "You practically beheaded him. That wasn't a smile, Frankie. That was like, 'Yikes! Don't throw anything at me again, you strange scary girl'."

Frankie's lip curled. "You're jealous, because I'm his type."

"What type is that, then?" inquired Kenny coldly.

"Quirky. Interesting." Frankie flicked her

dark hair so that it fell over one eye. "Enigmatic."

"Insane," Fliss suggested, giggling.

"Get real, Frankie," Kenny scoffed. "Didn't you see his scarf? Owen's a Leicester City fan, like me. Having stuff in common, that's what counts. Not enigmatic hair or whatever."

Fliss was studying her pastel-pink nails with their perfect half-moons. "My mum says boys prefer really feminine girls."

Lyndz snorted. "Dream on, sister! Didn't you see Owen's face when I was chatting to Natalie? I was telling her where I go horse-riding. And I could see he was really fascinated."

"Who's the liar now?" demanded Kenny. "You expect us to believe us that was a private chat? I mean, you weren't deliberately yelling at the top of your voice, so Owen would overhear it or anything?"

"No, I was not, Laura McKenzie!" said Lyndz angrily.

I stared at them open-mouthed. Had my friends gone raving mad?

OK, so I had a mushy True Romance

moment, when Owen first walked in. But to hear them talk, you'd think he was like one of those old portraits where the eyes follow you all around the room!

"Owen can't have been looking at ALL of you simultaneously. Unless he's got like, some major eye defect!" I pointed out.

"Clean your ears out, Rosie Cartwright!" snapped Frankie. "I told you. He wasn't looking at ALL of us. He was looking at ME."

"And I told YOU!" Lyndz snarled. "The poor boy was just cringing, in case you lobbed something else at him."

Kenny shook her head. "Guys, this is really stoopid."

I puffed out my cheeks with relief. My mates were finally coming back to their senses! "I agree," I said eagerly. "I mean, he's a boy, right? He's totally not worth all this—"

Kenny silenced me with an icy glare. "What I was going to say, before Rosie interrupted me," she growled, "is that all we have to do is PROVE which one of us Owen likes best."

"Oh, PERLEAZE!" I said. "Haven't you guys got ANY pride?"

But obviously they hadn't, because they instantly perked up.

"Kenz, you're right," said Frankie excitedly. "But who'll be the judge? We're going to need someone who's not, you know, personally involved."

"How about Rosie?" Lyndz suggested. "She's not the romantic type, are you, Rosie?" she grinned. "She's much too sensible."

"That's what you think," I muttered to myself. But out loud I said, "Hey, don't go dragging me into this, OK?"

But they totally ignored me. Kenny reached into her pocket and pulled out an old spelling book. She tossed it to me. "Here you are, Rosie Posie," she said. "There's some pages left. Keep score in that."

"Keep score of what, bird-brain?" I demanded.

They stared at me.

"I don't believe Rosie, sometimes. She wasn't even listening," Frankie complained.

"She's so selfish," agreed Fliss. "If it isn't about her, she just doesn't want to know."

I waved my hands in front of their faces.

21

"Hello! I'm still here, you know." But they totally ignored me. "Hey! How come *I'm* selfish, anyway?" I said huffily. "It's not *me* that's scratching my friends' eyes out over some stoopid boy."

"Pleeease, Rosie," Kenny coaxed. "We'll make it easy for you." She produced a stump of pencil. Then she leaned the spelling book against the wall and drew four roughly vertical lines down each of its spare pages.

"I'll write our names on the left," she explained. "Then I'll label these columns. Erm – Column One for if Owen smiles at anyone. Column Two for if he actually *says* something to one of us."

Frankie put on her fruity milkmaid voice. "And Column Three is for any like, *special* favours," she giggled.

Fliss's jaw dropped. "What kind of favours?"

"*You* know," smirked Frankie. "If Owen shows he really, *really* likes one of us. A LOT!"

Fliss fanned herself with her hand. "Oooer," she said.

"Cuckoo," I told them. "You're all completely cuckoo."

"Oh, go on, Rosie," everyone pleaded.

"You've only got to put ticks in boxes," said Kenny. "We're not asking you to donate a kidney."

"We'd do it for you," Lyndz added. "You know we would."

Don't you just hate it when your friends try to make you feel guilty?

"All right," I sighed. "But when it goes horribly wrong, don't say I didn't warn you."

"It'll end in tears, my lovelies," said Frankie in her sexy milkmaid's voice. "NOT," she added rudely.

After break, the Sleepover Club's fascinating love-life was forced to take a back seat, because Miss Pearson made an unexpected announcement.

"For the next few weeks we'll be doing a very special history project," she beamed. "We'll be studying the Second World War. More specifically, the Blitz."

Everybody groaned.

"No-one cares about that stuff now, Miss," Frankie complained. "If you ask me, it's time everyone got over all that old war business and started looking to the future." And she sneaked a little peep at dishy Owen!

He was nodding away, like he was in total agreement, but for all I knew a bee just flew into his ear.

I stuck up my hand.

"I agree with Frankie," I said. Because I did, actually. "This is the twenty-first century. Children of today should be focussing on peace, not war."

The other Sleepover girls clapped and cheered. At first I was chuffed that my mates were backing me up. Then I realised THEY were sneaking looks at Owen, too. They didn't give two hoots about me. They were trying to impress their blue-eyed boy!

"Good point, Rosie," said Miss Pearson cheerfully. "Except I'm not convinced that world peace comes about by ignoring huge historical events. Rather the reverse. We need to understand what happened, so we can make sure these things never happen again."

"Oh, wah, wah, wah!" said Frankie loudly. And she flicked her hair over one eye, purely for Owen's benefit.

Miss Pearson sensibly ignored her. "I can guarantee that you'll find this project really enjoyable," she went on. "It won't just be about facts and dates, you know. It'll be a hands-on experience."

Frankie's shoulders shook with phony laughter. "A hands-on experience of the Second World War!" she said scornfully. "How enjoyable is *that*!"

I'd slid so far down my chair, I was practically under the desk by this time. Frankie was *totally* embarrassing me! Personally, I don't see why a girl has to make a berk of herself to get boys to notice her. And if he DOES find that kind of obvious behaviour attractive, then he's simply not worth bothering with. That's what Mum says, anyway.

After school the others pestered me for an update on their scores. Fliss screamed like she'd sat on a pin when she realised she was in the lead. Believe it or not, she'd actually got a tick in the "Special Favours" column. (It wasn't for anything icky. Owen just gave up his seat for her at lunchtime!)

The others immediately got the sulks.

"I warned you this would happen," I sighed. "If you ask me, we should stop this *stoopid* point-scoring business right now."

But they wouldn't hear of it.

You know what, though? I know this makes me sounds like a major headcase, but after being madly in love with Owen Cartwright for like, two whole hours, I'd totally gone off him.

It wasn't just the depressing effect he was having on my normally sane and cheerful friends. It was Owen himself. He'd started to remind me spookily of somebody else. But I couldn't think who.

Incidentally, I got a good look at Mr Heart-throb as we were hurrying out of the school gates, and guess what? His smile wasn't nearly as mysterious and lovely as I'd thought. At close quarters, it was actually more of a creepy smirk.

Suddenly, I saw what should have been obvious from the start. Our point-scoring system was a waste of time. Because charismatic Owen Cartwright was already totally and helplessly in love.

With HIMSELF!

All at once, instead of being thrilled that we shared the same surname, it started to grate on me. Also, I'd found out that Owen was six months older than me. And it made me furious to think that this smirking boy had been a Cartwright for a whole six months before *I* came into the world!!!

But it wasn't until I was drifting off to sleep that night that I finally figured out who it was that Owen Cartwright reminded me of.

It was our deadly enemies, the M&Ms.

CHAPTER THREE

Let me quickly remind you that in the never-ending cosmic battle between good and evil, the Sleepover Club represents the Good Guys (YAY!!). Whereas the M&Ms definitely walk on the Dark Side (BOO! HISS!!).

OK, I'm exaggerating, but you get the picture.

The M&Ms' real names are Emma Hughes and Emily Berryman, otherwise known as the Gruesome Twosome. And they're in our class, worse luck. In front of grown-ups, they're as sweet as pie. Sweet, but seriously toxic. Their only aim in life is to get one up on *us*, the cool and groovy Sleepover crew. Though like

Kenny says, it beats her why two such incredibly CATTY girls are so desperate to be top DOGS!

Anyway, when I walked into the playground next morning, all the girls in our class were in little huddles. Their faces were shining with excitement. As I passed, I heard the same name, over and over. "Owen, Owen, Owen." It was like a horror film! I prayed that my mates, at least, had miraculously come to their senses in the night. But when I spotted them, round by the gym, they had that same distinctive Owen glow.

I soon learned that Owen's G (for Gorgeousness) Rating had just zoomed off the scale. Apparently, lover boy was way cooler than everyone thought. Not only were his parents stupendously rich. Not only had he just moved into the ritziest, glitziest house in Cuddington. But gorgeous Owen Cartwright himself was actually (GASP!) a professional boy supermodel!!

To be fair, the others weren't bothered about the house or the money. But they were totally gobsmacked by the supermodel thing. I hung around, listening to them witter. Now and then I'd say hopefully: "So about our next sleepover…"

But it was like I was invisible. It dawned on me that if I wanted their attention, I'd have to use the O-word. Like, "Hey, let's give our sleepover an Owen theme!" But I absolutely *refused* to join in the madness. So it was a relief when the bell went and it was time to go into school.

That morning, we had to start our Second World War history project, and the whole class was having a *major* sulk.

"You could let us do the Tudors, Miss," Fliss whined. "They had the coolest clothes."

Kenny's eyes gleamed. "Also the MOST beheadings!"

Kenny LURVES to gross everyone out. She *says* it's because she wants to be a doctor like her dad, but if you ask me, she's plain bloodthirsty!! Mind you, it was good to hear her sounding more like the pre-Owen Kenny, if you see what I mean.

"That does sound tempting," Miss Pearson grinned. "But I think we'll stick to my original plan. Bring your chairs to the front. I've got some things to show you."

The class scraped and scuffled its way to the front of the class.

To our surprise, Miss Pearson produced a small cardboard case from under her desk. "What do you think is inside?"she asked.

No-one had the least idea.

She lifted out some bizarre apparatus – kind of goggles with rubber tubes attached. "Like to make a guess what it is?"she asked.

"Diving equipment?" said someone.

Emma Hughes flashed a superior smirk at Owen, who instantly smirked back.

"Getting warm," smiled Miss Pearson. "It is a form of breathing gear. But for use on land."

A forest of hands went up. "Oh, Miss, Miss!" everyone pleaded.

"Ryan?" she asked.

"It's a kid's gas mask," he said.

Fliss is SO-O fickle! That girl has been in lurve with Ryan Scott for the longest time. But today she didn't even glance his way. She was too busy fluttering her eyelashes at You Know Who.

"That's right," beamed our teacher. "People thought this new war was going to be a complete re-run of the first one, when our enemies used poisonous gas. They were wrong, as it turned out. But everyone was issued with a gas mask. Even little children."

Miss Pearson passed the gas mask around, explaining that it originally contained asbestos and other dangerous substances. "But don't worry. It's been cleaned and it's quite safe," she said.

Of course Kenny had to try it on. "Peeyoo!" she choked. "It pongs."

There's no way I was putting that thing over my face. But Lyndz said it just smelled of rubber and disinfectant.

Incidentally, it took Danny McCloud all of five seconds to realise you could make a really rude noise by breathing hard into the gas mask!

The minute I heard that sound, I came out in goosebumps. I suddenly KNEW that those wartime kids were no different to us. I bet the first thing *they* did with their masks was make rude noises too, don't you?

"At the start of the war, children took their masks everywhere," Miss Pearson explained. "They actually had gas-mask practice at school."

"That must have looked well weird," Danny chortled. "Thirty-five little kids sitting around wearing these."

"Plus the teacher," snorted Ryan.

Everyone cracked up. But you could tell that people were starting to get interested in Miss Pearson's project.

"Did they take their masks when they were evacuated, Miss?" I asked.

"Does everyone know what Rosie's talking about?" Miss Pearson asked.

Everyone suddenly looked vague.

"When the war began, well over a million city children were sent away to the country," she explained. "The government wanted them as far away from air raids as possible."

Lyndz waved her hand. "That's like *Goodnight Mr Tom*, Miss! I saw it on TV. The kids had labels round their necks, like luggage."

"And they had sweet little Fair Isle jumpers," said Fliss dreamily.

"Not to mention fleas, nits and ringworm," grinned Miss Pearson.

"Ugh, Miss," protested everyone.

"It's true," she said. "Many evacuees came from extremely poor homes. Some of them had never even seen sheep or cows. The whole experience must have been very frightening. And they must have been desperately worried about the families they'd left behind."

Frankie turned pale. "Miss!" she gasped. "They didn't send babies away, did they?" Frankie's got this cute baby sister, called Izzy. She's so soppy about her, it's not true.

Miss Pearson looked sympathetic. "I don't think so, Frankie."

Next, our teacher showed us an actual ration book. I could almost *smell* the history on it. It was really worn, almost greasy with age, and the pages were totally dog-eared. It had belonged to some lady called Violet Chance in Bethnal Green, London.

Miss Pearson explained that during the war, even basic things like eggs were in short supply. "Rationing was introduced to make sure everyone got their fair share," she said. "But women still had to queue for hours to buy food for their families."

She waved a grim-looking recipe book. "The government employed experts to dream up bizarre new recipes, explaining how housewives could make cakes out of dried eggs instead of fresh ones, or how to use turnips instead of strawberries in jam-making."

"Euw," gulped everyone. "Gross."

"It gets worse," she said. "They tried to persuade people to eat whale or horse meat!"

Lyndz was horrified. "I would rather starve to DEATH than eat a horse," she said fiercely.

Everyone agreed with her there! Even the M&Ms drew the line at eating ponies.

Miss Pearson showed us other fascinating bits and bobs, including a pack of Happy Families, featuring wartime characters like Adolf Hitler! Finally she produced a small enamel pie dish with a tiny chip in it.

"What's so special about that old junk?" giggled Emily Berryman, fluttering her lashes in Owen's direction.

"I'll tell you," said Miss Pearson quietly. "It belonged to my great aunt. She'd only been married for three days when her husband was called up to fight overseas. This pie dish was one of the few things she'd had time to buy for their home."

"What happened?" said Fliss anxiously.

Miss Pearson smiled. "Don't look so worried. She rescued it from the ruins, after the house she was living in suffered a direct hit."

We passed the pie dish around reverently. Wow, I thought. I'm touching something that survived a bombing raid.

Miss Pearson announced that for anyone who was interested, she'd be cooking an authentic Second World War meal in the Home Economics room at lunchtime. As you can imagine, none of us was exactly crazy about the idea.

Then Danny grinned. "Oh, all right, I'll give it a go."

"Yeah, why not?" smirked Owen Cartwright, like he was doing Miss Pearson some huge favour.

"We'll come, won't we, Emma?" said Emily

Berryman at once. She has this funny gruff voice, like one of those teddy bears you tip upside-down.

My mates exchanged glances. No WAY were they leaving Owen to the tender mercies of the M&Ms!

"You can put us five down, Miss," said Frankie quickly.

I shook my head. "Not me."

"You've got to," hissed Frankie.

"Give me one good reason!" I hissed back.

Frankie pulled a face. "Because of that thing you've got to do. You know!" She nodded towards Kenny's old spelling book.

"Oh, that," I groaned.

"Is there a problem, Rosie?" asked Miss Pearson.

"No, Miss," I sighed. "I'll be there."

When lunchtime came, I trekked dutifully down to the Home Ec room with the others. Suddenly Fliss reversed madly down the corridor. "Ouf," she gasped. "It smells worse than Andy's mum's cabbage soup."

Unfortunately Miss Pearson saw us through

the open door. "Just in time," she called cheerfully. "I've started dishing up."

We were trapped!

It wasn't cabbage soup, as it turned out. It was something even more disgusting. Would you believe (gulp!) Dock Leaf Pudding? Those poor wartime housewives were so frantic to get vitamins into their kids, they'd even cook WEEDS!

Miss Pearson dished up gruesome little helpings for everyone, explaining that the pudding had been cooked in a "hay-box", a cunning wartime wheeze for saving fuel.

Here's how it worked. You started your stew, or whatever, on the cooker. When it was bubbling nicely, you took it off the stove and plonked it in your handy hay-box, which was a box packed with actual hay. (So *that's* why they called it a hay-box! Duh!)

In case you're wondering, the hay was to stop all that precious heat from leaking out, while your stew carried on cooking in the box. It acted a bit like a Thermos flask.

For those of you interested in a revolting culinary experience, here's the recipe.

> ### Dock Leaf Pudding
> Take young dock leaves and boil them in a pan with chopped spring onions. Add a handful of oatmeal, a beaten egg and a knob of butter. Simmer for half an hour.

(Serving tip from R.C. Now bury at the bottom of the garden and evacuate surrounding area!!)

Miss Pearson let us suffer for all of ten seconds. Then she gave a wicked grin. "However, I thought some of you might be allergic to dock leaves, so I brought some back-up," she said. She whipped open the oven door and produced a tray of yummy mini-pizzas.

Everyone gave sighs of relief. Then Miss Pearson nuked some packets of French fries in the microwave, and we got stuck into our REAL lunch!

As you know, I'm not the kind of girl to turn up her nose at free pizza. Nor would I DREAM of saying "I told you so". But would you believe that after we went to all that trouble, Owen didn't turn UP? Nor did the M&Ms.

"I smell a rat," said Frankie darkly.

"More like a frog," I mumbled.

My mates gave me funny looks.

"I was trying to think of something really slimy," I fibbed hastily. SomeONE really slimy, was what I actually meant!

We were heading for the playing fields, gulping big breaths of fresh air. After our close encounter with the Dock Leaf Pudding, we were desperate for extra oxygen.

But when we got there, who do you think was running round in his cute little shorts, merrily playing footie? And who do you think was cheering him on adoringly? Yep! Owen's latest fans, the M&Ms, plus their sad little slave, Alana Palmer.

My mates looked as if they'd just heard Christmas was cancelled. Personally, I thought they should have more pride. Plus I totally didn't want the M&Ms getting one up on us.

"Let's go," I pleaded.

But all my friends were gazing at Owen as if they'd never seen anything so awesome. It was like all they'd fallen under some evil SPELL.

I'm not that crazy about football, so while I waited for my ordeal to be over, I kept myself busy by collecting incriminating evidence against Owen Cartwright.

Would you believe that boy POSES every time he goes to take a penalty? He even pushes his hand through his hair, David Ginola style!

This was truly one of life's major mysteries. My friends were so SMART. Couldn't they see this bogus boy was unworthy of their affections? URGH! I thought. How DARE he have my surname!!

Suddenly I'd had it up to *here* with that fair-haired phony! I informed the others of my decision as we were walking home in the rain.

"All bets are off," I said crisply. "I refuse to help you guys make wallies of yourselves."

"You can't do that!" wailed Fliss.

"I just did," I scowled. And while I was feeling brave, I told them what I thought of Mister Charisma.

Frankie was furious. "Rosie Cartwright, if you weren't such a little fuddy-duddy, you'd know Owen's the best thing to happen to our school in *ages*."

"Rubbish!" I snapped. "Miss Pearson's history project is heaps more exciting than some – brainless HIMBO!"

I should have saved my breath. Even after I'd crossed the road, I could still hear my mates wrangling about which of them Owen liked best.

When I got home, I felt like a real Rosie No-Mates. Why couldn't I fancy Owen too? I thought miserably. At least I'd have something to giggle about with the others.

But once I'd seen the creepy resemblance between our school Romeo and those two-faced M&Ms, I couldn't NOT see it, if you see what I mean.

It was like that fairy tale in reverse. Inside Owen's princely good looks lurked a seriously icky frog in disguise, I was sure of it. I just prayed that sooner or later, my friends would come to their senses and see that I was right.

CHAPTER FOUR

The others must have agreed to stop going on about Owen – at least, when *I* was around anyway, because next day, they never mentioned him ONCE. Which was basically cool with me.

After registration, Miss Pearson got us buzzing with the news that some exciting visitors were dropping by later that morning, to help out with our history project.

In my opinion, "exciting" is a word teachers totally overuse. "Gosh, listen everyone! The school nurse is going to show this *really* exciting video about head-lice!" NOT. But Miss Pearson didn't strike me as the kind of person to get psyched up about nit shampoo, so I was genuinely intrigued by who these visitors might be.

While we were waiting, our teacher showed us some old photographs which had been taken in and around our part of Leicestershire during the Second World War. We were gobsmacked. Sixty years isn't that long, really, but it was hardly recognisable as the same planet!

The people looked as if they'd just stepped out of some crackly old black and white film. Plus there was almost no traffic. The few vehicles around were *total* museum pieces. Miss Pearson explained that petrol was in really short supply, so people only used cars when strictly necessary.

There was one photo of these three teenage girls. They were really pretty, in that well-scrubbed, healthy 1940s way. And something about their happy expressions made me think they'd be fun to know.

"How come they're so stylish?" demanded Fliss. "You said clothes were rationed, same as food."

"They were," Miss Pearson agreed. She explained that the war changed women's lives dramatically. Until then, they hadn't been encouraged to go out to work. But with the men away at war, women were needed to work in the factories or on the land. Some even joined the forces.

"Girls and women had to become much tougher and more independent," our teacher went on. "But despite all those wartime shortages, they were determined to look their best. If you look closely at this girl's pretty coat, you'll see she's made it herself out of a candlewick bedspread!"

"Oh, yeah!" breathed everyone. "Excellent!"

"In those days, girls thought it was amazingly cool to wear silk stockings with seams down the back," Miss Pearson grinned. "But they were hard to get, unless someone sold you a pair on the black market – illegally, in other words. So girls painted fake seams on their bare legs, with gravy browning."

Fliss's hand flew to her mouth.

"That's the bravest thing I ever heard!" she choked.

Everyone was still falling about laughing when there was a knock at the door. A buzz of excitement went round the room. Our mysterious visitors had arrived!

The door opened… And to our dismay, the secretary showed in two old ladies.

I know, I know! Don't give me that "All old people are not doddery" lecture. Like, some of them do yoga and belly dancing and go off backpacking to countries with no indoor plumbing, blah blah blah. And you totally don't need to remind me that when Madonna draws her pension, she'll still look incredibly sexy in leather trousers!

But I'm telling you about *these* old ladies, OK? So trust me when I tell you they were the kind you'd pass in the supermarket without a second glance. Everything about them shrieked "old lady": their handbags, their crinkly hairdos, those saggy tights which look like they're sewn together from bandages, and their clumpy sensible shoes.

You could see the whole class thinking, "WHA-AT!" I was thinking the exact same thing. As far as I was concerned, the words "exciting" and "old lady" had no right occupying the same sentence.

"I'd like to introduce Mrs Iris Liddell and Mrs Edith Cooke," beamed Miss Pearson. Even their names sounded kind of dusty, like they belonged in a museum along with all those comical old bangers.

My mates assumed polite expressions, preparing to be bored out of their minds. To my surprise, Iris and Edith exchanged glances. A kind of "oh-oh". I went hot and cold. *They know what we're thinking,* I thought.

Then it dawned on me. These old ladies might be able to read us like a book, but they didn't give a HOOT what we thought about them!

And quite suddenly, I sat up and took notice.

"Mrs Liddell and Mrs Cooke kindly agreed to come into school to share their wartime experiences," Miss Pearson explained. "And I must say, I'm looking forward to it enormously." And she came to sit down with the rest of us.

"Good morning," said Iris, in her crackly old

lady voice. "At this moment, you are all obviously wondering, 'Why in the world should we listen to these two prune-faced old biddies?'"

Everyone hastily stared at the floor.

Iris roared with laughter. "And quite right, too!" she said sympathetically. "There's nothing worse than listening to some old buffer rambling on. But sixty odd years ago, when war first broke out, my sister and I were not so prune-like. In fact, if I say so myself, we were pretty hot stuff!" And she twinkled at us over her bifocals.

Everyone giggled with surprise.

Iris held up a picture of two stunning girls dancing with two men in uniform. "That's Edith and me doing the jitterbug, the night Glenn Miller's Band came to Leicester," she beamed. "They were very popular at the time, rather like Boyzone now."

Boyzone? These old dears were talking about *Boyzone*?

"… and Edith and I danced the night away," continued Iris. "It was the last evening we spent together for some years. Next day my sister went off to work for a hush-hush outfit in Bletchley, known as Station X. Shortly afterwards, I joined the Land Girls, and learned to drive tractors and muck out pigs!"

In two minutes, Iris and Edith had got the entire class eating out of their hands. Prune-faced or not, they were stomping! Interrupting each other and cracking jokes, just like my mates in the Sleepover Club.

Edith, Iris's eldest sister, was this like, maths genius at school, which is how she ended up deciphering secret enemy codes at Station X. Then she was whisked off to Egypt on some mysterious mission, travelling in the bomb bay of a Lancaster bomber!

She showed us a picture of herself, taken in front of the Pyramids, looking frightfully English, in a floaty summer dress. Beside her was a handsome man in uniform. (The kind who just HAS to be played by Joseph Fiennes if they ever make the film!)

"Who was *he*?" all the girls said at once.

"Oh, Mungo was a spy," she said casually. "A double agent and a complete bounder!"

"Dishy though," Fliss whispered.

Sharp-eared Edith heard her. "Extremely dishy," she sighed. "But rotten to the core."

At first, Iris's war sounded tame in comparison with her sister's. She basically drove tractors, and baled hay. Now and then she'd get an enigmatic postcard from Edith and wonder what she was REALLY up to! Then, some German prisoners of war (POWs for short) arrived, to help out with the harvest.

Iris turned pink as she described how one of them made her laugh. His name was Helmut and he spoke very good English.

"Highly inconvenient," she said, "falling in love with the enemy! I longed to tell my friends how Helmut had rescued a baby rabbit from the combine harvester, or that he hated Hitler as much as they did. But I had to keep everything locked tightly inside me, until I thought I'd burst."

She paused and there was this electric silence. Everyone wanted to know what happened next.

Iris sighed. "Then, when the harvest was over, Helmut was sent to another farm in deepest Devon, and I didn't see him again."

"Not ever?" we gasped.

"Oh, yes," she smiled. "After the war ended, he wrote, asking me to come to Germany."

"Did you go?" asked Danny McCloud, totally caught up in her story.

"I did," she nodded. "And it was terrible. Helmut came from Dresden, which if you don't know, was badly fire-bombed by us. It was a place of absolute despair. I still dream about it."

"They deserved it, though, Miss," Alana piped up. "After what they did."

Iris gave her a sad smile. "I'm not qualified to decide who deserves to die horribly and who does not. I only know it was terrible. Everyone in Helmut's family had been killed, except his mother. She died soon after I arrived, and Helmut and I came back to England together."

"As you can imagine," said Edith dryly, "our parents were not exactly delighted."

"Our father never spoke to me again," Iris sighed. "Luckily my mother forgave me the instant she set eyes on our first baby."

I could have listened to those incredible Blitz sisters all day! Even my Owen-crazy friends were utterly spell-bound.

But just before Iris and Edith left, something AMAZING happened.

Edith explained that she and Iris owned a house which was maintained in perfect Second World War condition, like a Blitz time-capsule.

"It's only small," said Edith apologetically. "Which means only a few of you can participate at any one time."

"So we thought the fairest thing would be to set you all a competition," said Iris. "The lucky winners will get to spend a weekend in the Second World War!"

A ripple of excitement went round the class.

"A Blitz sleepover!" gasped Kenny. "I can't wait!"

"Me neither!" said Frankie. "This is one competition we've GOT to win!"

"Coo-ell," Lyndz and Fliss agreed.

"No question," I said.

Twenty-four hours ago, the Sleepover girls were totally anti-Blitz. Now we were all *desperate* to ace Iris and Edith's competition!

Miss Pearson asked us to give the sisters a big clap for being such total stars. A few people got carried away, whooping and whistling as if they were on *Ricky Lake*.

Danny McCloud actually asked for their autographs. "I've never met any spies before," he told Edith.

"I wasn't a spy, dear," she chuckled. "I was really just a number cruncher."

"Number *what*?" he frowned.

"What you'd call a computer nerd," she explained. "Except they hadn't invented computers then."

"Oh, I get you!" beamed Danny. "I'd still like your autograph!" he added cheekily. "I think you're really cool!"

At lunchtime, the Blitz competition was the sole topic of conversation.

"How do we make sure we ALL go?" wailed Fliss.

"Yeah, only some of us might win," agreed Frankie.

"Hmmn. Good point," mused Kenny.

At that moment there was a squeal of Minnie Mouse laughter. We looked up and saw a horrifying sight. Owen Cartwright and the M&Ms were at the SAME dinner table, laughing away like old friends!!!

I counted to ten, and took a sacred vow that the words "Told you so, you big wallies!" would never pass my lips.

Frankie jumped to her feet and stormed out. "That does it," she snarled when we caught up with her. "Those girls have gone too far! We've got to get them back BIG time."

We started thinking up satisfying forms of revenge, like zapping them with water-bombs, or sneaking opened tins of Whiskas into their PE bags. But Frankie rejected all our creative suggestions.

"The best revenge is for us to win the competition," she said fiercely.

Kenny looked doubtful. "Nice thought. Any idea how we pull it off?"

"Yes, actually," said Frankie smugly. "We'll submit a joint Sleepover entry."

"All *right*!" we all cheered.

"As individuals, we're the best," Frankie

beamed. "Think how awesome we'll be as a team!"

Wow, I thought. This is only happening because Owen was hanging out with the M&Ms. Mum's right. Things really DO happen for a reason!

I grinned at my mates. "Yeah," I said aloud. "We should be truly unbeatable!!"

CHAPTER FIVE

I had some serious brainstorming to do. So after I'd watched a bit of TV and had a little snack (or four!), I got stuck in.

The sisters had asked us to describe what we'd learned from our history project, and show how it related to our own lives. Should be a doddle, I thought. There's got to be LOADS of ways!

But the minute I tried to put even ONE down on paper, all my great ideas vanished in a puff of smoke.

After about an hour of mental torture, I rang Frankie. "How's the brainstorming going?" I asked.

"A total write-off," she yelled over Izzy's howls. "I can't hear myself think. My little sister's getting some new teeth!"

OK, I thought. Frankie's in Baby World. Let's try Fliss.

"I have NO idea how this is meant to work!" Fliss wailed. "I wouldn't paint my legs with gravy browning if you paid me and Mum would MURDER me if I cut up my bedspread and used it for a coat."

Fliss had got hold of the wrong end of the stick as usual, but I wasn't in the mood to argue, so I just told her to chill, and punched out Lyndz's number. Can you guess what was wrong with Lyndz? SURE you can!

"Can't talk now, hic, Rosie," she gasped. "I've got some serious, hic! hic! hiccups!!"

"*BOO!*" I yelled down the phone. But Lyndz's hiccups are not easily impressed, so I hit the TALK button and cut her off.

It's lucky I left Kenny till last, I thought. SHE won't let me down.

"Hiya, Kenz!" I said breezily. "How are you doing with the Blitz Sister thingy?"

Unfortunately Kenny was in a really bad

mood. I found out later that she'd had a HUGE row with her sister Molly.

"I'm not," she snapped. "Plus my rat went missing."

"Euw," I said. "Oh," I corrected quickly. "I'm really sorry."

Rats totally freak me out. Even tame ones like Kenny's. I think it's their tails that give me the horrors. But Kenny's crazy about hers (her rat, you wally! Not her tail!), so I tried to sound sympathetic. "Hope you find him soon," I croaked.

"I can't talk, OK?" Kenny said irritably. "I've gotta look for poor old Merlin." And she put down the phone.

"Gr-reat," I sighed. Instead of boosting my morale, my friends had totally depressed me. Maybe I should sleep on it, I thought. Maybe I'll wake up tomorrow, and go "Eureka! That's IT!"

But as it turned out, I didn't have to wait NEARLY that long. Because, just as I was helping my brother Adam with his tea, I had this BRILLIANT brainwave.

I didn't write it down then and there. First

Adam had to finish eating, then I had to check out my idea with my mates. But when the others heard what I had to say, they were over the moon.

"Coo-ell," whispered Frankie. "You're the best!" (I assumed she was whispering because they'd finally got Izzy to sleep.)

"MAJOR breakthrough," said Fliss admiringly. "The M&Ms are going to be GREEN!"

"I'm v. impressed!" said Kenny. "And so's Merlin. Would you believe he was cuddling up to Molly's old Barbie in the garage? Isn't that cute?"

"Euw," I said faintly. "Yes, really cute." (NOT!)

Lyndz was finally hiccup-free, so she was in an excellent mood. "Go for it, Rosie," she said gleefully. "Knock their socks off!!"

So I went for it. It still took me ages to get it right. But by bedtime, I'd got our entry completely sorted. This is what it said:

Nowadays we have this stupid idea that some people aren't as useful as others. It's like you're meant to fit into this tidy category, and if you don't, you might as well be invisible.

For instance, if you're too young, that's not useful. But if you're too old, that's just as bad. And if you've got some kind of disability, FORGET it!

Well, during the war, people in this country couldn't afford to think like that. Everyone had to do their bit. And I mean EVERYONE, from little kids to housewives to wrinkly old grandads.

And that's how it is in my house. Without my dad, things are sometimes tough going. But everyone pulls together and somehow it works. People seem to think my brother Adam doesn't contribute anything to our family, because of his cerebral palsy. But they're SO wrong.

It's the same with my mates in the Sleepover Club. They'd have been brilliant during the Blitz, because each of them has something really special to contribute.

Frankie would keep everyone entertained with her jokes and silly impressions. Fliss would make sure all our clothes were mended, and that everyone was scrubbed squeaky clean. Kenny would run around stacking sandbags, and collecting old pots and pans to be recycled into bombs and aeroplanes. And Lyndz would have been a land girl like Iris, helping out on farms and looking after the horses.

Miss Pearson's history project taught us that wars aren't just about fighting. They're also about getting the best out of people in a crisis, and everyone playing their part, however small. And from this point of view, the Sleepover Club girls would have been total stars!

Next day, my mates read my entry in absolute silence. I got more and more nervous. They hate it, I thought.

I was about to make a run for it, when I saw they'd all gone red.

"It's rubbish, isn't it?" I said miserably.

Frankie shook her head. "It's beautiful, Rosie," she said softly. She actually had tears in her eyes. Then she flipped her hair behind her ears. "Erm, did you mean it about me being funny and entertaining?"

"I meant what I said about ALL of you," I said truthfully.

"That's SO sweet!" breathed Fliss.

"It's brilliant, Rosie!" beamed Kenny. "You're a genius!"

"It's all down to Adam, really," I said. And I made up my mind that if we won, I'd give my brother an extra squeezy hug!

Everyone read it through once more for luck, then we all solemnly signed our names, to show that this was an official Sleepover Club entry. Then we marched up to Miss Pearson's desk and handed it in.

As we went back to our seats, Frankie stuck her tongue out at the M&Ms. She said she totally couldn't resist!

Then just as I sat down again, it hit me! BAM! This was all MY idea. So if we lost the competition it would be MY fault! To make things worse, Iris and Edith would be judging all the entries.

I started getting all knotted up inside. I know it's stupid, but I was totally desperate for Iris and Edith to like us best out of everyone in the class. I wanted to get to know those feisty Blitz sisters better and have a laugh with them in their funky time-warp house. And the more desperate I was for my dream to come true, the more I was convinced I'd blown it.

By the time I got home, I didn't know what

to do with myself. I'd been banking on my brother giving me some SERIOUS cheering up. I'd totally forgotten he was staying at Dad's.

So I rushed off to Mum. She looked up from her books, and at first I thought she was really listening. But as I burbled on, I realised she was just making those vague mum-noises. You know the kind. "Yes, Rosie. No, Rosie. Oh, you must be feeling absolutely terrible, Rosie."

"So I thought I'd just go and boil my head," I said in my most neutral voice. "And then hack off all my limbs one by one."

"Yes, you do that, sweetheart," said Mum soothingly. "And ask Tiff to defrost some lasagne for tea, would you?"

So I went to watch TV with my sister Tiffany.

My sister's not the most sensitive girl in the world, but even *she* guessed something was wrong when I burst into tears in the middle of a McDonalds commercial. (It was that one where the little children cover their sleeping dad with their entire collection of Beany Babies.)

"All right, Rosie," she sighed, "What's bugging you now?"

Tiff goes on like I'm always working myself into a froth about nothing. When *she's* the family member who deserves her own personal soap opera. Still, I was desperate, so I blurted out all my worries.

"It's our one and only opportunity to have a genuine Blitz sleepover," I sniffled. "But it's all down to me. And I can't handle that much responsibility. If the M&Ms win, the others will never forgive me!"

To my surprise, Tiff really understood what I was going through.

"When I was at primary school I had some deadly enemies *just* like Emma and Emily," she grinned.

"Yeah?" I said. "Did they sleep in lead-lined coffins?"

She giggled. "Me and my mates were ALWAYS trying to get one up on them. But if they won, it was like the world had ended."

"I know what you mean," I sighed.

"The funny thing is, Pippa's one of my best mates now," Tiff said casually.

My mouth fell open. "You're kidding!" I breathed.

"It's true," she said. "We've got absolutely loads in common."

I held up my hand. "Don't even go there," I said fiercely. "There is no WAY I will ever have anything in common with those mutants."

"OK, OK," said Tiff. "But you shouldn't let them get to you. You should do the best you can for yourself and your friends, not worry about them." She ruffled my hair. "Trust me," she said affectionately. "I know what I'm talking about!"

I hate to admit it, but my sister was talking sense. It would be great if we really could flatten those Goody Two-Shoes with our combined brilliance. But what mattered was, I'd given it my best shot. With a whole week of waiting ahead of me, I clung bravely to this thought.

After our chat, we had a really mellow evening. Eventually Mum finished her college work and the three of us sat around stuffing ourselves with supermarket lasagne and watching TV.

They had one of those *Auntie's Bloomers* programmes on. And for about the gazillionth time we laughed till we cried, at those poor *Blue Peter* presenters skidding around in all that steaming elephant poo.

But that night I found myself remembering what Tiff said about her ex-enemy, Pippa. As you can imagine, the idea of becoming best friends with the M&Ms was deeply scary.

It wouldn't be SO bad, I thought, if it happened when we're all very old, like Iris and Edith. Or maybe if Cuddington was invaded by space aliens, plus all the other humans were like, DEAD.

Yeah, and if Emma and Emily had total personality transplants, I told myself. Or if someone hypnotised us. Get real!

I cuddled up to my duvet in the dark. Nah, I though happily. Don't even think about it, Rosie Cartwright, because it's never going to happen!!

CHAPTER SIX

I've never been too sure what "tenterhooks" are, have you? I picture them like those serious steel hooks you get in butchers. But whatever they are, all week, the Sleepover Club was TOTALLY dangling from them, longing to know if we'd won.

Miss Pearson prolonged everyone's agony by keeping the result under wraps until the afternoon. When the big moment came at last, everyone looked extra-alert. OK, maybe not everyone. Owen was doing his "I'm so deep" smile. And the M&Ms just looked annoyingly smug, like always.

"They make me SICK," fumed Lyndz.

"Do you mind not using that S-word?" I gulped. The tension was getting to me and I was worried I might lose my lunch for real.

Fliss gave my hand a loyal squeeze. "You'll always be the winner in my eyes, Rosie," she whispered.

Miss Pearson looked up. "Right," she beamed. "I'm sure you're dying to know the results of our Blitz competition."

She waved an envelope. "Iris and Edith told me that they read all your entries with great interest. But apparently one entry stood out as exceptional."

The M&Ms gave squeaky Minnie Mouse giggles and hugged each other. We rolled our eyes. Those girls are SO unbelievable!

Miss Pearson tore open the envelope. "Let's see who has won the unusual honour of spending the whole weekend in the Second World War," she grinned.

"This is like the Oscar nominations," hissed Frankie.

Miss Pearson slid out a piece of paper and gave a mysterious smile. "And the winner is…"

My tummy totally looped the loop.

"THE SLEEPOVER CLUB!" she beamed.

Kenny punched the air. "YAY!"

Did I mention that we'd agreed to play it really cool if we won? Yeah, right! We went totally crazy, jumping up and down and hugging each other, and screaming our heads off.

The M&Ms looked as sick as parrots (heh heh heh!). Owen just gave a bored shrug, as if this whole Blitz sisters thing was way beneath him.

But we totally didn't give a hoot!! From Saturday through till Sunday, we'd be living in 1940s Britain. It was going to be one of our coolest, most unusual sleepovers ever, and as you know, we've had quite a few!!

When I woke on Saturday, I knew we were going to have the BEST time. It was one of those sparkly bright days, the kind which makes you zingy and happy inside.

Iris and Edith had provided us with heaps of 1940s gear beforehand. So when they came to collect us, they found five little 1940s waifs waiting for them, wearing Fair Isle cardies, pleated skirts and woolly socks held up with garters! Not to mention pixie hats and coats. (Luckily, our gruesome 1940s underwear didn't show!)

Fliss's mum took this snap of us. Don't we look AMAZING? Can you see we've got labels round our necks, like real evacuees? We've even got cute old-fashioned suitcases. The clunky cardboard cases over our shoulders are our gas masks, if you're wondering. Incidentally, Fliss's mum insisted on doing our hair in proper 1940s hairstyles, and I think it made all the difference.

We didn't just LOOK different though, we had totally new identities too. Miss Pearson had given us new names, which were like, typical for girls at that time. Plus we all had authentic Blitz life-histories.

I was Audrey Harris (that's actually what's written on my label, but it doesn't show up in the snap). My mum worked in a munitions factory (where they made bombs and stuff). My dad was away fighting in the Middle East with some army outfit known as the Desert Rats.

Frankie's 1940s name was Dorothy, and she

had the WORST life history. Just about everyone in her family had died, except for her poor old granny. Frankie was thrilled to bits. She is SUCH a drama queen!

Lyndz and Kenny were meant to be sisters, which they thought was quite cool. Mind you, Kenny was less than thrilled when she found out her Second World War name was Daisy!!

"Eek, that's WAY too girly! Can't I swap it with Lyndz?" she pleaded.

"You actually WANT to be called Betty?" giggled Lyndz. "You sad, sad girl!"

Would you believe Fliss had to be someone called Ruby Goodbody! "How come I always get the stoopid surname?" she wailed. "First Sidebotham, then Proudlove, now this!"

I forgot to tell you Iris and Edith had dressed in 1940s costume too. Far more thrillingly, they'd actually arrived in a genuine old-fashioned car!!

Our mums and dads had come to see us off. But I'll tell you something weird. As we drove away with the Blitz sisters, I saw Mum, Tiff and Adam waving like crazy. And my eyes filled up with tears! I felt exactly like a lonely evacuee who didn't know if she'd ever see her loved ones again. Get a grip, Rosie, I told myself. Then I saw that all the others were furiously blinking away tears. Even Kenny!

Of course, Frankie had to go WAY over the top.

"I'll never see my old bed-ridden granny again!" she sobbed. "How will she get down to the air-raid shelter without me?"

Luckily, before things got out of hand, Edith started to sing in her crackly old lady's voice. It was a song called *We'll Meet Again*, which was really popular during the war.

Lyndz gave Kenny a watery grin. "Come on, sis!" she said. And they joined in the singing.

"That's the spirit," said Iris briskly. "Chin up."

We swallowed our tears and sang along at the tops of our voices. This must be what they mean by the Blitz spirit, I thought. And it really brought it home to me, how tough people had to be in those days.

I forgot to tell you that the Blitz sisters' time-warp house was on the other side of Leicester. In actual miles, it's not that far. But I've got to say, that car ride was the most bizarre journey

I ever had in my LIFE!

I mean, I knew I was still in Rosie Cartwright's century. I only had to look out of the window to see that. By the time we reached Leicester, there were like, THREE lanes of traffic, crammed with cars and buses and lorries, all zooming along at speeds which would have turned Audrey Harris to jelly. And overhead, rooftops bristled with TV aerials and satellite dishes, which were *definitely* not around during the 1940s.

Also, in Audrey's day, English people mostly came in one colour – white! But in present-day Leicester, you meet people from everywhere in the world. Plus you can buy a zillion yummy kinds of food: Chinese, Indian, Japanese, Jamaican, Thai, you name it. Poor Audrey probably had to plough through icky macaroni cheese and stewed mutton and sad veggies with all the vitamins boiled out of them. (They weren't too clever about vitamins in her day.)

Anyway, like I said, I knew I was still in my own century. Yet here I was, chugging along in that old-fashioned car, feeling Audrey's clothes prickling against my skin, and bursting with weird emotions which TOTALLY weren't mine.

It was like, the minute I put on my evacuee clothes, I'd split into two different girls – the twenty-first century me, and a 1940s version. It made me feel MOST peculiar.

We chugged up a little back street, and stopped outside a tiny house with sandbags outside. There were wartime posters plastered around, telling people to DIG FOR VICTORY, and *not* to leak crucial info to spies (CARELESS WORDS COST LIVES).

We all got out and Iris fetched our suitcases from the boot.

"Welcome to the Living Blitz Experience," beamed Edith.

I followed her inside and found myself in a brown-painted hall, standing on bare, highly-polished lino. A serious shiver went down my spine, as if I really had stepped back in time. Then I caught sight of Frankie's face.

Only, for that split second, she wasn't Frankie. She was a bewildered evacuee, clutching a battered little suitcase. And I'm not lying, I went completely weak at the knees.

"This feels well weird," whispered Kenny.

Lyndz patted her cheek. "I'll look after you, sis!" she grinned.

We tiptoed from room to room. There was no carpet, just more shiny lino and (very slippy) rugs, so our footsteps echoed like mad. We were truly gobsmacked at the lack of mod cons.

For a start, the loo situation was *unbelievably* basic. You had to go OUTSIDE to use it. And instead of nice soft toilet paper, there was horrible hard shiny stuff. The toilet did have a flush, but you just *knew* there were sinister creepy-crawlies lurking behind the pipes.

Plus, there was NO central heating. There wasn't even an immersion heater for baths and washing up. As for power showers, electric kettles, videos, TVs or computers, FORGET it!

"But what did people do for FUN?" asked Fliss in bewilderment.

Edith came in behind us. "They listened to the wireless," she smiled. And she showed us a genuine Second World War radio. It was the size of a giant hat box, and was made out of a clunky old-fashioned plastic called bakelite, if you like technical details!

"What did they listen TO, exactly?" asked Frankie doubtfully. "I mean, did they even have pop DJs then?"

Edith laughed. "I'm afraid not. People listened to the news a great deal, obviously. And comedy shows were a big favourite. There was one called ITMA. You heard ITMA catchphrases everywhere in wartime."

Iris appeared in the door. "Like TTFN," she beamed.

"What does *that* mean?" spluttered Lyndz.

Iris and Edith giggled like kids. "TaTa For Now," they chorused.

"Is that like ' See ya'?" asked Kenny.

"Exactly like that." Edith grinned at her sister. "They've been asking me what 1940s girls did for fun."

"Amused themselves, mainly," said Iris. "You might like to see these."

She showed us piles of 1940s games, plus stacks of comics and magazines. We had a great time flicking through old film mags.

Kenny noticed that the female stars were more, well – SOLID than our present-day versions. "They look so healthy," she said admiringly. "Like they've just been playing netball, or something."

The male heart-throbs were way too smooth for our taste, not to mention ANCIENT! Everyone agreed that none of the 1940s guys came anywhere near Leonardo diCaprio for gorgeousness.

By the time we'd finished playing Hunt the Heart-throb and a couple of games of wartime Happy Families, our lunch was ready.

"It smells OK," said Kenny cautiously.

Edith dished up a savoury fry-up of mashed potato, onion, and cabbage with crispy bacon bits mixed in.

"Bubble and squeak," she beamed. "I know that, erm, Dorothy is vegetarian, like Iris, so we also cooked a vegetarian version."

We all got stuck in. Except for Fliss, who only picked politely around the edges. She told me later that she was freaking out about consuming so many calories.

And it's a good thing I was hungry, because

we had steamed treacle pudding and custard for afters!

"No WONDER those film stars were on the chubby side," Fliss whispered, when Edith and Iris left the room.

"They probably needed the stodge to keep them warm," shivered Kenny.

"I'm going to burst," groaned Lyndz. "I just want to laze around and watch TV."

"Uh-uh," said Frankie. "No TV, remember?"

But after we'd helped with the dishes, Iris and Edith said we were going to do some lessons.

"At the weekend?" Frankie gasped. "Is that even legal?"

I thought 1940s school sounded fun. But I quickly changed my mind. Back then, lessons consisted of chanting tables, copying maps and learning things by heart, including (AARGH!) poetry!! I had to learn a poem which went, "*The boy stood on the burning deck whence all but he had fled*" or something like that. Don't laugh! It's by someone really famous, OK!!

We were all shocked to realise how little

equipment schools had then. And they had a really pitiful supply of books. Even paper was rationed during the war – isn't that awful?

"Wow," breathed Frankie. "When I get back to the twenty-first century, the first thing I'm going to do is kiss my computer!"

You'll never guess how we spent the rest of the afternoon. Iris and Edith taught us how to KNIT!! It sounds really fogey, but knitting was HUGE during the war. Everyone was doing it, even big blokes and little kids. They didn't just knit for their relations, they did it for soldiers and the ambulance service and bombed-out families.

Fliss decided to make a scarf. No prizes for guessing what colour wool she chose. They really should have called that girl Barbie! Lyndz and Kenny went for the scarf option too. Kenny's was in Leicester City colours – no surprises there, then!

Frankie wanted to knit a pair of gloves, but the sisters thought that was a TEENY bit ambitious, so she made a scarf too. Unfortunately they didn't have any silver wool (Frankie's got a real thing for silver, as you know), so she chose some lurid rainbow-striped stuff instead.

I started on a cosy balaclava for Adam in royal blue. To my surprise, I didn't drop *that* many stitches.

Lyndz's scarf looked more like a doily, but then she DID have an attack of hiccups in the middle. Anyway, the sisters said we'd all done REALLY well for beginners, so we were quite chuffed with ourselves.

By the time our knitting lesson was over, it was time for tea. I was secretly hoping that "tea" meant home-made scones and fruit-cake. But it was basically a cup of milky tea with some slices of bread and margarine. I really, really HATE that old-style margarine, don't you?

Then to our horror, Iris and Edith announced that it was bedtime.

"But it's only seven o'clock!" gasped Lyndz.

"Children went to bed earlier in those days," said Iris firmly. "Anyway, by the time we've boiled kettles for you all to wash, it'll be seven-thirty."

She was right. Boiling a kettle on a gas ring

takes FOREVER. Plus, washing at the kitchen sink was an experience I could totally have done without.

Suddenly Fliss went pale. "What if we need the loo in the night?" she shuddered.

"I'm going to cross my legs till morning," announced Frankie. "If you've got any sense, you'll do the same."

"I can't wait that long!" wailed Fliss. "I've had too many cups of tea. If I don't go soon, it'll come leaking out of my ears!"

"Honestly, Fliss, you nutcase!" giggled Lyndz.

"Don't worry," said Kenny sweetly. "We'll come with you." Her expression was unusually innocent.

After we'd all washed and brushed our teeth, we trooped off with Fliss to use the (ahem!) facilities, one last time. For some reason, Kenny took ages.

"Sorry," she said breezily, when she finally came out. "Couldn't get it to flush for ages."

It was time to go upstairs to our freezing cold bedroom. We were in the same one, luckily. Frankie and Kenny had to share a wonky iron bedstead. The rest of us had the big double bed.

When I took off my socks, the lino felt icy under my bare feet.

Lyndz's teeth were chattering. "I'm keeping my vest on under my jim-jams," she shivered.

Everyone thought this was a sensible idea. But we couldn't WAIT to take off our liberty bodices. They're these padded things which children wore OVER their woolly vests, and UNDER their shirts and cardies. I don't know why they called them liberty bodices. Mine made me feel totally trapped!

Our bed swayed about like a boat every time anyone moved. Instead of a duvet, we had sheets and blankets and a shiny eiderdown, which slithered around as if it had a mind of its own.

The pillows had real feathers inside, except that some of them weren't. Inside, I mean. They poked out through the pillowcase, like little spikes, and if you weren't careful they gave you a nasty jab in the face.

It took us a good couple of hours to settle down. I was just drifting off to sleep, when the bedroom door flew open.

To my horror, I could hear the eerie wail of a siren coming from somewhere. Someone shone a torch into my eyes. It was Edith, wearing her coat over her nightie.

"Get some clothes on!" she said urgently. "We've got to go down to the shelter!"

And suddenly I wasn't Rosie Cartwright any more. I was an evacuee, in the middle of an enemy air-raid. And I was taking part in the Blitz experience for real!!

CHAPTER SEVEN

We dragged our coats over our night things. My fingers were shaking with fright. I was convinced I could hear enemy planes droning overhead.

Lyndz hates to put her shoes on in the dark. She worries that spiders might have crawled inside while she wasn't looking. So she went to switch the light on, but Edith snapped, "No lights after sunset, dear, you know the rules."

I remembered Miss Pearson saying how they didn't allow street lights during the war, in case enemy pilots spotted them from the air. People had to put up special "black-out" curtains, to stop the lamplight shining out into the street. Air-raid wardens patrolled the streets yelling, "Put that light out!" if anyone disobeyed.

It suddenly hit me how stressful it must have been, stumbling about in the dark, for night after night after night...

We followed Iris and Edith out into the garden.

The night sky was cloudy, and it was drizzling. The kind of night which makes slugs and snails ooze out from under their stones and groove happily around the garden, making icky slimy trails.

The idea of treading on slugs and snails normally freaks me out. But at this particular moment, I wasn't nearly so scared of squishing slugs underfoot as I was of being caught out of doors in an air raid. My mouth was literally dry with fear.

Suddenly, we all froze in the middle of the garden.

We'd just seen the shelter.

"Rosie," whimpered Fliss. "I can't do this!"

"But it's just a mound of earth!" gasped Frankie.

"Nonsense, it's a perfectly good Anderson shelter, dear," said Iris calmly. She glanced up and I heard an edge of fear in her voice. "Quickly now, everyone inside!" she barked.

I glanced up too, and saw the lights of a plane directly overhead. A flash of terror went through me and I dived into the shelter.

It wasn't too bad once you got inside, though it did smell rather damp and earthy. The shelter was kitted out with camp beds and warm blankets. Plus, to everyone's relief, there was a storm lantern.

Iris struck a match. There was a hissing sound and a little yellow flame sprang up. A pale wobbly light filled the shelter.

Suddenly I noticed an ominous-looking bowl. A horrible thought floated into my mind.

"What's that for?" I asked casually, praying it wasn't what I thought it was.

"That's the chamber pot, dear," beamed Iris. "In case anyone needs to go in the night."

Fliss gave a stifled wail. Frankie just firmly crossed her legs.

We all sat around rather awkwardly, not knowing what to say.

It was past midnight by this time, but for some reason I wasn't tired. But I was REALLY peckish!

Suddenly Kenny's tummy gave a ginormous rumble. "I'd kill for a packet of crisps," she muttered.

Luckily, the groovy Blitz sisters were prepared for all emergencies. Edith started to unpack a little picnic from a wicker basket. No crisps, disappointingly. Just a flask of hot cocoa, some home-made jam tarts and some sandwiches. But it was *très, très* welcome, believe you me!

Iris had brought a pack of Animal Snap (an authentic 1940s pack, naturally!). And for the next hour or so, the only sounds were the comforting hiss of the lantern, plus a total uproar of baa-lamb bleats, piggy grunts, moos, etcetera. Also our mad giggles, obviously!

"That'll give the enemy something to think about," giggled Kenny. "Hearing *those* noises wafting up into his cockpit!"

For some reason that made everyone crack up. Iris and Edith laughed till they cried. Their giggles were wickedly infectious. Before we knew it, we'd all collapsed into one of those marathon giggling fits, the kind which leaves everyone feeling exhausted, but stupidly happy at the same time.

Frankie wiped her eyes. "You two are now honorary members of the Sleepover Club," she told the sisters. "You passed the giggle test!"

"Why, thank you," said Iris, looking really touched.

"That is a true honour," agreed Edith.

But before things could get too mushy, Iris burst into a stirring Blitz-type song, and we all joined in. Wow, I thought. We're actually having a genuine wartime singsong, like the ones Miss Pearson told us about!

Luckily, 1940s songs are simple to pick up. Soon we were belting out *You Are My Sunshine* and *There'll Be Bluebirds Over The White Cliffs of Dover* and other songs popular back then.

Eventually we felt brave enough (and tired enough!) to go to bed.

Kenny yawned loudly. "Think I'll get my head down," she said.

Lyndz gave me a nudge. "Hope the sisters

don't snore," she whispered.

"Sssh, they'll hear you," I hissed.

Iris and Edith tactfully waited until we were tucked up in our camp beds, before they turned out the lantern. Then the shelter was plunged into inky darkness. I couldn't even see my hand in front of my face!

"It must have been really scary for the kids doing this for real," I said. (I was feeling more like my normal Rosie Cartwright self by this time.)

Edith's voice came out of the dark. "It was. Very scary."

Lyndz's camp bed creaked as she sat up in the dark.

"Is that why you run this Blitz experience?" she blurted. "So people will understand what wars are like?"

There was a pause, then Edith sighed. "This is only a *little* taste of what a real war is like, dear," she said.

"But it is one reason," agreed Iris. "Also we don't want people to forget what very extraordinary times they were."

After a while, everyone went quiet. I didn't

see how I was ever going to get to sleep. I was shattered, but my brain was totally buzzing.

Suddenly Fliss's camp bed boinged madly as she jumped out of bed. "AARGH! Something's crawling on my face!" she shrieked.

Trust me, these are not words you want to hear when you're lying in total darkness inside a Second World War shelter!

Of course, me, Lyndz and Frankie immediately leapt out of our beds, screaming like maniacs. I heard the quick scrape of a match, and once again the shelter filled with wobbly lantern-light.

Kenny sat up, rubbing her eyes. "What's all the fuss?" she mumbled in a drowsy voice. "I'd just dropped off then."

Edith and Iris exchanged glances. "Hmmn," said Edith to Iris. "Our little Daisy's just a bit too sweet and innocent, wouldn't you say?"

Frankie's eyes narrowed. "Kenz!" she barked. "What's that empty matchbox doing next to Fliss's pillow?"

Fliss yelped and knocked it to the floor.

"Yeah, sis," said Lyndz suspiciously. "What

have you been up to?"

"You *didn't* smuggle in some creepy-crawlies," I said. "You wouldn't!"

Kenny's face split into a grin. "Heh heh heh," she chuckled. "Just because a girl's got a soppy name, doesn't mean she's a total goody-goody!"

We glared at her.

Kenny rolled her eyes. "Honestly, it was just a baby earwig, you guys. I could've got something MUCH bigger and nastier. That outside loo is full of them!"

"I don't care," Fliss whimpered. "The earwig could be anywhere by now. I'll be awake all night!"

"No, you won't," I told her. I pointed to what looked like an ex-earwig, very sad and squished on the floor. Fliss must have flattened it when she jumped out of bed. Everyone inspected it carefully to make sure it was dead. But Fliss totally refused to go back to bed until the earwig corpse had been put outside the door. Then she forced us to check the soles of her feet for any earwig remains. Finally Edith snuffed out the lamp again.

I couldn't see how I'd EVER go to sleep after so much ruckus. But I must have been tireder than I thought. All at once, daylight was streaming through the open door into the shelter, and I could hear a bird singing at the top of its voice. I'd survived my first ever actual air-raid. (And hopefully my last!)

The sisters had gone back to the house to organise breakfast.

Kenny rubbed her eyes. "Ouf," she said. "I don't know about you guys, but I couldn't handle that kerfuffle every night!"

"Huh," Fliss mumbled darkly.

"The Blitz kids didn't have a choice," I pointed out.

"That's true," yawned Lyndz.

Frankie hugged her knees. "I tell you what," she said sheepishly. "I totally believed in that air raid, last night. I felt like I'd really and truly gone back in time. Isn't that dumb?"

It turned out we'd all felt exactly the same. For those few electric minutes, we'd got totally caught up in being our wartime selves. And Edith and Iris's impressive play-acting skills (and their authentic Blitz sound effects!) had done the rest.

Our night in the shelter had made us all really hungry, so we trotted eagerly back up the garden and into the house.

I wasn't too impressed when Edith announced that we were having porridge. I'd only had porridge once and it looked like something you'd use to glue wallpaper. But Iris and Edith's porridge was dee-licious! I had no idea oatmeal could taste that good. Plus it REALLY fills your tum!

After a bracing wash (boy, cold water wakes you up FAST!), we put our prickly clothes back on and went to help Edith weed the garden.

We weren't very clued up on which were plants and which were weeds, unfortunately, so we just whipped out the obvious ones, like bindweed and dandelions.

"You're growing loads of veggies," said Lyndz admiringly.

"Food was in short supply during the war," Edith explained. "People used every inch of space to grow their own. Even parks and playing fields were dug up and turned into gardens."

"Why was it called the Blitz anyway?" asked Kenny suddenly.

Edith smiled. "It comes from a German word, *blitzkrieg*, which means 'Lightning War'. The Germans intended the war to be as swift and fierce as a lightning strike. They bombed British cities almost every night for a year, trying to batter them into submission."

"That's why I was evacuated, isn't it?" said Frankie. Then she blushed. "My character, I mean," she said hastily.

Edith told us other surprising facts. Like, did you know Buckingham Palace was hit by a bomb? Because I had NO idea!

Also, the Germans were dropping incendiary bombs – bombs designed to start fires. At one point, there were *1400* fires raging through the city of London!

"It must have smelled horrible," shivered Lyndz.

"It did," said Edith. "It also meant enemy pilots could see London from the air, even at night, because it was lit up like a huge bonfire."

"How did people BEAR it?" I breathed.

"Because they had no choice," said Edith.

"Also because very ordinary people are sometimes quite *extraordinarily* brave."

After we'd done the weeding, we helped Edith pick some vegetables. Iris was making veggie soup for lunch. We took them into the kitchen, and Iris immediately got us scrubbing and chopping their home-grown leeks and spuds.

"Life was very hard work then, wasn't it?" sighed Lyndz. She was rinsing leeks under the tap, and it was taking ages.

"I suppose it was," Iris agreed.

Edith plunked some more muddy vegetables in the sink. "But we did have an awful lot of fun!" she said mischievously.

Kenny looked doubtful. "Did you *really*?" she asked.

The sisters' faces lit up. "Oh, YES, dear!" they breathed.

Edith's eyes twinkled. "Let's show them, Iris," she said.

They led us into the sitting room, giggling like naughty girls. Edith rolled back the rugs. Iris took an ancient LP record out of its sleeve and put it on an old-fashioned turntable.

"This is called *In the Mood*," she beamed. "And it's played by the Glenn Miller Band."

Brassy 1940s dance music filled the air, and to our utter amazement, Edith and Iris began to dance. And I MEAN dance. Those sisters really went for it!

"Is that the jitterbug?" Frankie shouted, over the sound of the band.

"Certainly is!" Iris called breathlessly. "Want to try?"

And those fabulous Blitz sisters spent the next half-hour happily teaching us to jitterbug, foxtrot and quickstep.

Finally Iris remembered our soup and hurried away.

Lyndz collapsed on a chair. "I'm all in," she giggled, fanning herself with her hand.

"That was like a total work-out!" Fliss puffed.

"But did you have FUN?" grinned Edith.

"Yeah, actually," I said. "It was cool."

"Wartime dances *were* wonderful," Edith sighed.

"I bet," giggled Fliss. "All those good-looking spies!"

"It was a strange time," said Edith. "We

were so young. Yet we knew we could die at any moment. I suppose that's why people married in such a hurry in those days."

"I was wondering," said Fliss shyly. "How did they manage for wedding dresses? I mean clothes were rationed, right?" Fliss's mum got married in the summer, and Fliss is still heavily into weddings!

"If they had any sense, they didn't bother," yawned Kenny. "If I thought I was going to die next day, I'd just drag on any old thing. I mean, if you're just going to BLEED all over it!"

"No way!" Fliss objected. "I'd want it to be incredibly romantic."

Edith gave her a sympathetic smile. "A lot of wartime brides would agree," she said. "A friend of mine made a wonderful wedding dress out of parachute silk."

Fliss's eyes shone. "That is SO thrilling!" she breathed.

"Of course, it was impossible to have a traditional wedding cake," Edith went on. "Eggs were like gold in those days."

"What did they do?" giggled Kenny. "Make a papier mâché one, or something?"

Edith's eyes sparkled. "Almost!"

We stared at her. She was serious!

"People hired splendid cardboard replicas," she explained. "They *looked* like the ultimate dream wedding cake. Beautifully iced and decorated with a tiny bride and groom perched on the top."

"What's the point of cake, if you can't eat it?" scoffed Kenny.

Edith smiled. "Actually, the fake cakes had a hidden drawer."

"What was inside?" asked Fliss.

"CAKE, you nutcase!" we all yelled.

"That's right," chuckled Edith. "One teeny postage-stamp-sized slice of genuine wedding cake."

Which is exactly the kind of weird detail I would never have found out about, if we hadn't gone back in time with the Blitz sisters.

Our home-made soup was ready by this time. Personally I'm more of a tinned-soup girl. But I *quite* enjoyed the Second World War kind. Maybe because I helped pick and chop all the soup veggies myself.

*   *   *

After lunch, Iris and Edith drove us back to our waiting parents. This time the trip seemed to be over in a flash. I didn't quite know what to say to the sisters, now we were back in our own century, so I gave them both a shy little hug and rushed over to Mum.

"You're quiet," she said, as we drove home. "Didn't you have a good time?"

I leaned my head against her shoulder. "I had a great time," I told her. "The best."

When I got home, I rushed up to the bathroom and ran myself a bath. I splashed in tons of my sister's incredibly expensive bath stuff (I'm strictly forbidden to use it, which only made it all the more luxurious!!). Then I stepped out of my prickly Blitz clothes, and submerged myself in hot scented water. Aaah! Pure bliss.

After my bath, I put on some comfy clothes and went in search of a nice little snack. Then I curled up on the sofa with the TV remote and my knitting. Since our trip back in time, we're all totally nuts about knitting!

As you can imagine, I was seeing my mod cons in a whole new light. There's a lot wrong with the twenty-first century, I thought contentedly. But it's MY century, and it rocks!

Before I went to bed, I folded up my 1940s clothes. When I got to the coat, I felt something rustle inside the pocket. It was my evacuee luggage label. I traced my finger around the letters of my Second World War name. "Nice knowing you, Audrey," I murmured.

I put on my nightie and cuddled down under my duvet. The friendly glow of a street-lamp peeked between my curtains. I could hear Mum and Tiff downstairs, laughing at the TV.

Wow, I thought. I have such a great life! I don't have to worry about bombs or black-outs, or food rationing.

Not many people get a chance to be a completely different person for a whole weekend. Probably even fewer people get to travel back in time.

I badly wanted to say a special thank you to Iris and Edith for giving us such an amazing experience. But all I could think of was flowers, which was WAY too corny.

Hang on, I thought suddenly. I won the competition! Why don't I hand this problem over to the others, and get a good night's sleep?

So I did!!

CHAPTER EIGHT

I don't mean to get personal, but I bet there's times when you toss and turn worrying about like, *everything* in the universe. Am I right?

Well, here's some advice from Auntie Rosie. Get yourself down to Iris and Edith's WW2 time-capsule house, right now! I'm not saying I'm totally cured, but since my weekend with the Blitz sisters, I have practically resigned from my post as chief Sleepover Club worry-wart. And believe it or not, this laid-back approach WORKS!

Once I'd have stayed awake all night, brainstorming ideas for a special thank-you present for the Blitz sisters. Instead, I caught some serious Zs. And when I woke up, I didn't just feel wonderfully rested, I felt totally serene! I floated happily through the house saying, "Hello lovely Cartwright family members!", "Hello TV!", "Hello, comfy clothes, soft furnishings and friendly central heating radiators!"

Then it dawned on me. Since my weekend as Audrey Harris, all my old Rosie-type worries had just like, VANISHED!

Here's a typical old-style R.C. worry. "Oh, woe! Will my lovely hard-working mum ever get together with anyone in this lifetime? Or will she just be this lonely single person for ever and ever?"

Don't tell the others (it's kind of private), but I used to fret about this sort of stuff non-stop. It's SO-O tiring, like holding up the sky all by your lonesome. But that morning I just KNEW that none of these worries could COMPARE with the spine-chilling horror of looking up and seeing a sinister plane overhead, just about to drop bombs on everyone I love...

I went off to school, thinking my new

improved thoughts, catching up with the others at the gate. To my surprise, Fliss was glowing with excitement.

It turned out, *she'd* been wondering how to thank the Blitz sisters, too. But guess what? Fliss had also come up with the perfect solution!

"But I can't tell you yet," she said apologetically. "I'm not being funny, OK? I've just got to clear it with Miss Pearson first."

Fliss and Miss Pearson whispered in a corner for AGES, while we looked on, dying of curiosity. Then the plot REALLY thickened, because Miss Pearson suddenly announced that she was excusing Fliss from class for "a very special mission".

Fliss trotted off, looking incredibly self-conscious. She didn't appear again until lunch break.

"Come on, spill those beans!" Frankie commanded, as Fliss joined us at our table.

Fliss glanced round cautiously. "Not here, OK!" she hissed.

"Spies at ten o'clock," muttered Kenny.

We followed her gaze and saw the M&Ms

eyeballing us suspiciously.

As soon as we'd bolted down our lunch, Fliss dragged us off to a secluded corner of the playground, and unveiled her Big Idea.

Kenny's eyes gleamed. "Wow! That is so wicked!"

"Stomping," agreed Frankie.

"You're a total star, Fliss," I told her.

I meant it. She'd come up with the coolest thank-you idea ever.

Hey, keep your hair on! I'll tell you what it was in a minute, OK!

First I want to see if you can guess. Here's a couple of TINY clues. Fliss's radical idea involved:

1. A great deal of red, white and blue crepe paper.
2. A large tin of Spam. (No, I'm deadly serious!)
3. A number of old records.
4. And the letters V and E are HIGHLY significant.

I sound like mystic Meg , don't I!!

Yesss! Fliss wanted to give Iris and Edith their very own Victory party – a small-scale version of those cool street parties people had in 1945, to celebrate the end of the war!

Luckily, Miss Pearson was totally up for it. The party was scheduled for Friday afternoon. So we had almost a week to get ready.

With our teacher's help, we transformed our classroom with red, white and blue streamers. (Now you know why we needed all that crepe paper!) We also hung up dozens of little Union Jacks.

Our teacher baked a special V.E. cake, a HUGE one, and decorated it with groovy red, white and blue Union Jack icing. (V.E. means Victory in Europe, by the way.) Everyone agreed to bring in 1940s party food, including Spam sandwiches (aaargh!), little fairy cakes, jam tarts and sausage rolls. OK, maybe sausage rolls aren't authentic, but what's a party without them, right?

Anyway, hang on to your gas mask, because I'm going to fast-forward through the preparations, and cut to the actual party.

Our class really did the Blitz sisters proud!

Almost *everyone* had dressed in period style, starting with Miss Pearson, who had actually put her hair up in something called a "snood". That's a fancy hair-net, to you and me. I'd never heard of them, but Fliss said snoods were a MAJOR fashion statement back then. Our teacher even made her face up in period style – in other words, zero eye make-up, lots of pale powder, and LOADS of glossy red lipstick! She looked totally fab!

"You look exactly like those film stars in the sisters' film mags," Fliss told her admiringly. "Only not so chubby," she added quickly, in case Miss Pearson thought she was being cheeky.

Even the boys got into the V.E. spirit in a big way, greasing their hair into side-partings and wearing hand-knitted sweaters with those tragic 1940s boys' shorts. They look even sadder with Nike trainers. But who knows, it could be THE look for next season! Did I tell you Ryan kindly offered to be our party DJ, and provide authentic '40s sounds?

Owen was the only boy who refused to join in the general party mood. He just lounged in

107

the background, doing his sulky supermodel pout. But I noticed that my mates still stole longing glances at him.

Suddenly Danny yelled, "They're here, they're here!"

A familiar vintage car came chugging into the playground.

Fliss went pale. "What if they HATE my party?" she fretted. "What if they think it's really naff?"

Panic is SO-O catching, isn't it? We held our breath, waiting for the knock on the door. And finally, it came.

Miss Pearson snapped her fingers. "Now!" she mouthed.

Ryan punched a button on the stereo, and our classroom filled with big band music. Tingles went down my spine. And for a split second, I was Audrey Harris again, a scared human parcel with a label around my neck.

Then the door opened and Iris and Edith walked in – with two cute little toddlers, both clutching Furbies. The sisters stared around our classroom in amazement.

"You did all this for us?" Iris breathed.

"You *dear* children," said Edith in a husky voice.

Just then, one of the toddlers saw the food. "Oooh, goody! Cake!" she shouted happily. Everyone burst out laughing.

Yes, as you probably guessed, Fliss's V.E. party was a V. BIG success!! Everyone bopped and boogied to the mellow sounds of Glenn Miller, Tommy Dorsey and Victor Sylvester. We also played loads of silly games like musical chairs and charades.

The toddlers turned out to be twins. Their names were Harvey and Alice, and they were Iris's *great*-grandchildren, which made them precisely one-eighth German.

"It's so-o perfect that Iris brought them along," Frankie said earnestly. "Because the horrors of the Blitz are now totally in the past, and those beautiful little kids are like, our planet's future." Frankie always has to go way over the top, but for once we all agreed with her!

Incidentally, those little twins absolutely LURVED everyone in the Sleepover Club. They kept dragging us off to get them more fairy cakes, burbling away in toddler-speak, like they'd known us for ever.

Then the M&Ms tried to muscle in, going, "So what's YOUR name, you little sweeties?" in icky voices, and making a fuss of their Furbies.

Poor Alice and Harvey totally freaked out. They went scurrying back to Iris, wailing, "Go 'way! Not your sweeties. Not!"

"Dad always says toddlers have more sense than grown-ups," chortled Kenny.

"Yeah," agreed Frankie. "They saw through the Gruesome Twosome in a FLASH!"

By the way, the M&Ms looked like they were loving our Victory party as they jitterbugged frantically in their '40s outfits. But if you knew the signs (and BOY do we know the signs), you could see they were spitting with rage inside!!

Suddenly Miss Pearson signalled to Ryan to turn down the music. She clapped her hands to get everyone's attention. "Everyone having a great time?" she asked.

"Yess!" yelled (almost) everyone.

"Good! Because you've all worked extremely hard," Miss Pearson beamed. Then she picked up a large leather-bound book.

"Durn durn DURN!" sang Danny McCloud. "Iris and Edith, this is YOUR life!"

Miss Pearson grinned. "This class has been collecting people's memories of the Second World War," she explained to the sisters. "They also acquired copies of wartime photos taken locally. We put them in this special book, together with our own writing and artwork on the Blitz." She did one of her Oscar-ceremony pauses. "We'd like to present it to you with our heartfelt thanks for all your help!"

The Blitz sisters looked so touched, I was absolutely certain they were going to burst into tears. Edith quickly pulled herself together. "We'll treasure it," she said briskly. "And thank you for this wonderful party."

"It was Fliss's idea," Kenny blurted out.

Fliss went bright red. "Actually, it was Mum's," she confessed. "She always says, there's nothing like a party to say thank you!"

Frankie gave me a nudge. "And the Sleepover Club does LURVE to party!" she giggled.

Suddenly the door flew open and this glamorous woman wiggled in. She wore a low-cut dress the colour of vanilla ice-cream and girly shoes with incredibly high heels. A pair of trendy sunglasses perched in her wavy blonde hair. She wagged her finger at Owen. "I've got a bone to pick with you, you naughty boy," she cooed. "Keeping Mummy waiting all this time!"

Our mouths fell open in amazement.

Owen's mother flashed Miss Pearson a dazzling smile. "So sorry to interrupt your little party," she cried, "but my son has to be at an incredibly important photo-shoot in half an hour!"

Owen looked furious. "I told you I'd meet you out the front, OK?" he hissed at her.

His mother burst into peals of fake laughter. "Now, now, give Mummy a proper smile," she said playfully. "You won't get any modelling work pulling that sulky face!"

"Just get off my case, will you?" Owen jumped up and stormed into the corridor.

"Boys!" his mother sighed. "Who'd have them?" And she went tiptapping frantically after Owen on her high heels.

"Will you STOP moaning on?" we heard Owen whinge. "Anyway, you shouldn't wear that dress. It makes you look really old and fat!"

My mates stared after him. They looked completely dazed, as if they'd suddenly woken up from a long and rather strange dream. They'd finally realised that Prince Owen was a slimy frog after all.

Lyndz swallowed. "Erm," she croaked. "I have an important announcement. My humiliating crush is finally dead and buried."

Kenny looked queasy. "Ditto," she said.

Frankie nodded. "Yeah," she said huskily. "Next time I fancy someone, it'll be an actual person. Not someone's sad little pet poodle."

Lyndz giggled. "Give Mummy a proper smile, you naughty boy!" she spluttered.

I noticed Fliss hadn't said a word.

"What about you, Fliss?" I asked cautiously. "Do you still fancy Owen?"

She looked scandalised. "Don't be *stoopid*! I went off him AGES ago!" And she went back to gazing fondly at Ryan Scott.

That was totally music to my ears. "Thank goodness for that!" I sighed. "It was like, you were all possessed by the evil LURVE demon!"

My mates cracked up laughing, and suddenly they were all hugging me and jumping up and down and howling, "Yuck! Ugh! Gross!! How come we EVER fancied him?!"

The M&Ms glared at us through narrowed eyes. It's their meanest (and commonest) expression. They'd given up pretending to have a ball by this time. I gave them a cheery wave, which only made them madder than ever, heh heh heh!

Then I took a giant bite out of my yummy Union Jack cake. And as I watched Iris's great-grandchildren jitterbugging happily to a funky Glenn Miller tune called *Little Brown Jug*, I wished with all my heart that revenge could *always* taste so sweet!!

CHAPTER NINE

That night we held our regular sleepover at my house. But first my mates went home to collect their kit, plus the usual stash of goodies.

Normally, I rush around like a headless chicken, fretting about the tragically unfinished state of our house. But this time I just chilled out in front of the TV. ("Hello lovely TV!") So I was surprised to get a really bizarre phone call from Frankie.

She sounded like she was having hysterics. "You are not going to believe what I've just found out!" she yelped. "This is SO the end of the line for Owen Cartwright!!" Then her voice

115

changed. "Izzy, don't put that in your mouth!" And she clunked down the phone.

That is so typically Frankie. Can you believe she'd rung everybody in the Sleepover Club? Then, having made us wild with curiosity, she refused to say a single dicky bird while Mum and Tiff were around.

Tea was total *agony*. We were dying to hear Frankie's scandal, but everyone felt they had to be polite to Mum – you know how it is.

"So let's hear about this wonderful Blitz weekend!" Mum beamed. "Rosie's hardly said a word about it."

"It's really difficult to talk about," Frankie explained. "It's more like, you had to be there."

"It's something you feel!" Kenny agreed.

"Yeah," giggled Lyndz. "Like hiccups."

And we all giggled like total idiots.

Mum had borrowed the video of *The Parent Trap*. No-one wanted to hurt her feelings, so we sat through an hour and a half of like, total Hollywood fluff. It was quite good fun, though!

But at last we were up in my lovely room, putting on our night-things. ("Hello, twenty-first century jimjams! Hello cosy duvet!")

Mum came up to say goodnight. "You're very quiet," she said suspiciously

"Oh, don't worry about us, Mrs Cartwright," said Lyndz at once. "I expect we're just tired after all the excitement."

"Hmmn," said Mum, who is nobody's fool. She switched off the light.

We listened to her footsteps go downstairs, then everyone switched on their torches.

"Right!" said Kenny at once. "What's this juicy gossip?"

Frankie's eyes gleamed in the torchlight. "It's not gossip. I've got hard evidence!" She unfolded what looked like a page torn from a magazine.

"What's that?" asked Lyndz.

"I'm getting to it, OK?" (Frankie ADORES being the centre of attention!) "My mum gets this catalogue, right?" she began. Then she collapsed into giggles. "I'm sorry. It's just SO funny!" she choked.

"*Frankie!*" everyone yelled. "Spit it out, will you!"

Frankie's voice was wobbly with laughter. "It's not one of those big catalogues that sells everything," she quavered. "It specialises in this like, fogey thermal underwear. Mum gets it for my grandad. But apparently you can buy thermal stuff for like, ALL ages." She bit her lip, desperately trying to keep a straight face.

We stared at her. We had NO idea why Frankie was wittering about underwear catalogues. But we hung on in there.

"Well, you know how my baby sister likes to put everything in her mouth?" she went on.

"Ye-es," we said patiently.

"OK, so Izzy got hold of this catalogue, and naturally I took it off her. And look who was inside! Da da!!"

Frankie waved the torn page cheekily under our noses.

"Omigosh," gasped Lyndz.

"It's Owen!" breathed Fliss.

We fell about, shrieking with laughter. Well, you've got to admit that thermal underwear IS quite a comedown for a guy who goes around pretending to be a catwalk superstar.

"Wait till everyone hears about this," chortled Kenny. She was actually crying with laughter.

118

"Oh, come on, you guys," said Lyndz suddenly. "Let's just forget about him. I want to write in my Sleepover diary!"

"Me too," said Frankie.

The room was silent while we all scribbled away.

Frankie pulled a face. "I'm going to read what I put, OK? But I'd better warn you, it's about Owen. Here goes.

"'Owen Cartwright has finally been knocked off his lurve pedestal and it's weird'," she read aloud. "'First I thought he was like, this effortlessly cool guy, like someone in a boy band. Then I thought he was "rotten to the core", like Mungo, Edith's dishy spy. But actually, Owen's just an ordinary kid who's stuck with an incredibly gorgeous face.'"

"Plus he's stuck with Nightmare Mom," Lyndz smirked.

Kenny pulled a face. "They totally deserve each other!"

"I feel sorry for him," said Fliss. "You can tell the modelling is all her idea."

"So what!" objected Kenny. "He should stand up to her!"

"Erm, can I read mine? It's about the Blitz sisters," I said shyly. "It's only short."

"Good," grinned Kenny. "I'm getting well peckish."

I started to read. "'Since we did the Blitz experience with Iris and Edith, I can't look at old people in quite the same way. I used to switch off the instant I saw those wrinkly faces in the supermarket. But now I find myself wondering what hair-raising stories they could tell me.'"

"Yay!" said Kenny as soon as I stopped for breath. "Let's eat."

It was a seriously twenty-first century sleepover feast – not a Spam sandwich in sight! This is what we had: a big box of chocolate tea-cakes (our latest craze), a massive bag of potato hoops, a bag of jelly bears (OK, so we're sad!) and a packet of luxury chocolate-chip cookies, the double chocolate kind (because we're WORTH it!).

When everyone was full, we did a few rows of Blitz knitting, just to keep in practice. Poor Lyndz's looks even MORE like a doily now, but she's so proud of it, no-one can bear to tell her!

Finally, we had one last 1940s singsong (a very soft one, so Mum wouldn't hear). Then we switched off our torches and settled down to sleep.

But my head was buzzing with complicated thoughts. Like, how different our lives would be, if it hadn't been for the war. Apparently, until war broke out, girls and women were pretty much kept inside the home, either as servants, or like pretty ornaments for the men to admire. (Yeah, right!)

But when their country needed them, those ornamental women amazed everyone by doing just about everything men could do! I mean, nowadays we just take it for granted that girls can play football, like Kenny, or that mums go out to work. But if it wasn't for the war changing people's attitudes, these things would be like, *totally* unknown!

"Penny for your thoughts," whispered Fliss suddenly.

I grinned at her in the dark. "I was thinking how cool it is being us," I told her. "What about you?"

"I've just decided I'm going to put this really

sweet fringe on my pink scarf," she whispered back. "It's going to be like, FIVE different kinds of pink! I can't wait!"

Isn't that so typically Fliss? There's me, being really deep, and Fliss is having this Big Fashion Moment!!

Eek, is that the time? I had no idea I'd been nattering so long.

Look, I truly hope you enjoyed our Blitz sleepover, but if you don't mind, I've got to finish off Adam's balaclava before I get some shut-eye.

I forgot to tell you what? Are you SURE? Boy, you've got a good memory! You mean, I actually left myself out of that competition entry about team work and the Sleepover Club and stuff? How amazingly modest of *moi*! OK, let me think. Why would Rosie Cartwright have been a good person to have around during the Blitz...?

Well, I know it sounds boring, but I think being the sensible member of the Sleepover Club would have really come in handy. I mean, I'm still a BIT of a worrier (I'm not like,

TOTALLY cured, sadly!), but I'm basically a calm, optimistic person. Which you had to be back then, with bombs raining down, night after night.

Anyway, how sweet of you to ask! I'm touched. Plus I'll let you into a secret. I always lurve talking to our Sleepover fans, but this has been really special, kind of like talking to my mates. Let's meet up again really soon, OK?

And till then, TTFN!

34

Sleepover Girls in the Ring

Roll up, roll up, the circus is in town! When Ailsa the circus girl comes to Cuddington Primary, the gang are up for some serious fun when they sort out circus lessons. But whose crazy idea was it to juggle jam doughnuts in Fliss's house? The Sleepover Club is in BIG trouble – and things just get worse when they discover that Kenny's monstrous sister Molly is going to have circus lessons too!

Stick on a red nose and cartwheel over!

BUMPER EDITION!

Merry Christmas, Sleepover Club!

Cinderella is the school panto this year! The question on everyone's lips is – who will get the lead role? Fliss is hopeful, but there's a dark horse in the race who might beat her to it. And surprises all round for Rosie when her mum finds her own Prince Charming! Will everyone live happily ever after, or will the curtain fall on disaster?

Ho! Ho! Ho! for the Sleepover Club!

Collins

www.fireandwater.com
Visit the book lover's website

FREE GIFT ATTACHED!

Order Form

To order direct from the publishers, just make a list of the titles you want and fill in the form below:

Name ....

Address ....

....

....

Send to: Dept 6, HarperCollins Publishers Ltd, Westerhill Road, Bishopbriggs, Glasgow G64 2QT.

Please enclose a cheque or postal order to the value of the cover price, plus:

UK & BFPO: Add £1.00 for the first book, and 25p per copy for each additional book ordered.

Overseas and Eire: Add £2.95 service charge. Books will be sent by surface mail but quotes for airmail despatch will be given on request.

A 24-hour telephone ordering service is available to holders of Visa, MasterCard, Amex or Switch cards on 0141- 772 2281.

Collins
An *Imprint* of HarperCollins*Publishers*